Laura

Mary

Laura

Mary

To sit Baby Carrie in her
cradle, position the stand
backwards so the points
of the stand face forward.

Ma

Ma

Baby Carrie

Baby Carrie

Meet Laura

Once upon a time a little girl named Laura lived in the Big Woods of Wisconsin in a little house made of logs. She lived in the little house with her Pa, her Ma, her big sister Mary, her baby sister Carrie, and their good old bulldog Jack.

Doing Chores

Every day, Laura and Mary helped Ma wash the dishes and make the beds. After this was done, Ma began the work that belonged to that day. Each day had its own special work. Laura liked the churning and baking days best of all.

In the Garden

a, Laura, and Mary gathered potatoes and carrots, beets and turnips, cabbages and onions, and peppers and pumpkins from the garden next to the little house.

Helping Pa

Laura helped Pa get the little house ready for winter by gathering little pieces of wood. She filled her apron as full as she could of the little wood chips that fell to the ground as Pa chopped logs for the fire.

Baking with Ma

When Ma baked bread, Laura and Mary each had a little piece of dough to make into a loaf. Sometimes Ma gave them a bit of cookie dough to make little cookies.

Going Visiting

Sometimes Laura would go with Pa, Ma, Mary, and Carrie through the Big Woods to Grandma and Grandpa's house. In the winter the air was frosty cold, so they had to wrap up snug and warm for the trip ahead.

After Supper

After supper Pa would take down his fiddle and sing. He would keep time with his foot, and Laura and Mary would clap their hands to the music.

Bedtime

At night the little log house was snug and cosy. Pa, Ma, Laura, Mary, and Carrie were comfortable and happy in their little house in the Big Woods.

Insert this into the slots on the indoor side of the pull-out scene to change the scene from day to night.

To put Baby Carrie to bed, stand her up behind her cradle.

Jack

Pa

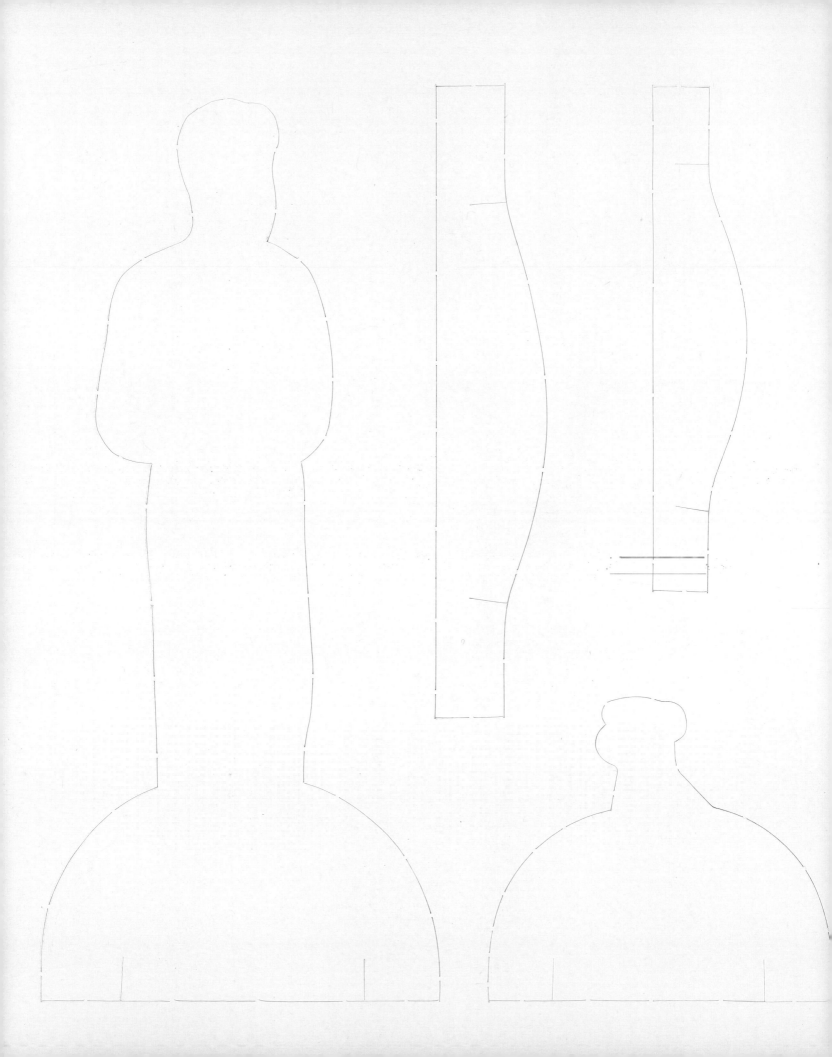

Insert the bread, book, pitcher, or bowl found throughout the book into the slot on this table.